CW00839317

Postman Pat's Foggy Day

Story by **John Cunliffe** *Pictures by* **Celia Berridge**

from the original Television designs by **Ivor Wood**

ANDRE DEUTSCH

First published in 1982 by
André Deutsch Limited
105 Great Russell Street London WC1
Second impression January 1983
Third impression June 1983
Fourth impression March 1984
Fifth impression May 1984
Sixth impression January 1985
Seventh impression October 1985

Phototypeset by Tradespools Limited, Frome, Somerset
Printed in Great Britain by Cambus Litho, East Kilbride, Scotland

British Library Cataloguing in Publication Data
Cunliffe, John
  Postman Pat's foggy day.
  I. Title
  823′.914[J]   PZ7

  ISBN 0-233-97473-3

There was thick fog in Greendale. Postman Pat had to go slowly along the winding lanes.

"This is nasty," said Pat.

Jess fluffed up his fur; he didn't like the fog either – it made a cold and clinging wetness in the air.

Pat was late when he reached the village post-office. Mrs. Goggins was busy dusting the shelves.

"Good morning, Mrs. Goggins!" called Pat. "Sorry I'm late – it's this blessed fog."

"No need to hurry," said Mrs. Goggins. "There's no sign of the letters yet. The fog's made you late; it will make the letters late, too. Come in and sit down, and have a cup of tea."

Pat went into Mrs. Goggins' sitting-room, at the back of the shop. There were big armchairs and a blazing fire. Pat warmed his hands and sat back amongst the cushions. Jess curled up near the fire and purred.

"I'll just brew up," said Mrs. Goggins.

"Thank you," said Pat; "this is lovely."

Pat was just getting warm and comfortable, and Mrs. Goggins was just bringing the tea and biscuits, when PING went the shop's door-bell.

"It's early for a customer," said Mrs. Goggins.

"That's a good cup of tea," said Pat. But Mrs. Goggins came in with the mail-bag, saying, "It's here!"

Pat was surprised. "What already? Just as I've picked my favourite biscuit, too. No time for that, now. I'd better be on my way. Come on, Jess."

He went into the shop and helped Mrs. Goggins to sort the letters. Then out into the fog again, and Pat was on his way. He knew the Greendale roads well enough, but they looked different in the fog.

He went the wrong way somewhere, so he stopped to look at a signpost. But it wasn't a signpost; only a crossroads sign. Now what? Pat didn't know which way to go. He walked along the lane, trying to see where he was.

Then he saw someone standing in the field. He said, "Why is he so still? It must be Ted Glen, out after rabbits. He'll know the way. I'll pop over with his letter and ask him."

Pat walked across the field very quietly, so as not to frighten the rabbits away.

He touched Ted on the shoulder.

Ted didn't move.

He put the letter in Ted's pocket.

Still Ted did not move.

He gave Ted a nudge.

Ted swung round suddenly! Oh! It wasn't Ted at all! It was a scarecrow. Pat did feel silly. He said, "Sorry, scarecrow, the letter isn't for you, and I don't suppose you can tell me the way in this fog. Goodbye!"

Pat walked back to the road. He was wondering what to do, when he saw lights coming through the fog. It was Alf Thompson on his tractor. Luckily, *he* wasn't lost; he soon showed Pat which way to go.

Pat was on his way again. His next stop was at the church. The Reverend Timms met him at the door. He said, "Hello, Pat. Isn't this fog ghastly! I don't know how you find the way. It's choir-practice, too. I expect Miss Hubbard will come; nothing stops her. Three letters, to-day? Thanks, Pat. Now go carefully, and trust in the Lord. Goodbye!"

"Cheerio, Reverend."

When Pat looked in his van, Jess had gone! He looked everywhere – under the van, behind the van, over the wall. There was no sign of Jess. Where could that cat be? He called – "Jess! Jess!" There was no answer. Perhaps Jess had gone looking for rabbits? Pat set out to seek him.

He called and called and called –

"Jess! Jess! Where are you?" He went over a stile, and across a field; through a gate, through a small wood, into another field, calling all the time, "Where are you, Jess? Jess! Jess! Come on, Jess. Here, puss: silly puss – this is no time for hide-and-seek."

He sat down on a tussock to rest. He put his hand on something furry. It moved!

"Oh!" What a fright it gave him. It was Jess!

"Jess, you silly cat. Where have you been?"

Jess was cold and wet; Pat could not be too cross with him. He gave him a cuddle, then tucked him under his arm, saying, "Come on, Jess. We'd better be on our way. Now, let's see, which way is it...?"

Pat was lost again and the fog was thicker than ever.
"Now you've done it, Jess. We're really lost this time."
Pat began to wander about in the fog. He couldn't find the road, let alone his van.
He walked into mud, up to his ankles.

Then he stumbled through a stream and a patch of nettles. The branches of a tree scratched his face and knocked his hat off. The fog swirled round him. He was lost, and more surely lost with every step.

Not so very far away, Miss Hubbard was cycling along the road. When she saw Pat's van, she stopped and looked inside.

"No Pat? No Jess?" she said. "I wonder if they are in the church?"

There was only the Reverend Timms in the church, sorting out the hymn books.

"Hello, vicar," said Miss Hubbard. "Have you seen Pat? His van's outside, and there's no sign of him or his cat. Whatever can have happened to them?"

"Dear me," said the Reverend Timms. "Pat called some time ago. They must be lost in the fog."

"I know what we must do," said Miss Hubbard. "We must ring the bells to guide them back to the church."

And that is what they did. They pulled the ropes, and the bells clanged and clamoured in the church-tower.

Out in the misty fields, Pat stopped to listen.

"Bells?" he said. "I thought it was a *choir*-practice. I wonder what they're ringing for? They're as good as a fog-horn. We'll soon find the way, now."

Pat followed the sound. The way went through a bramble-patch and some *very* prickly gorse; but it wasn't long before he found the road, then his van, then the church.

The church door opened, and in came Pat, blinking in the light.

"There's Pat!" cried Miss Hubbard, and they stopped ringing.

"Hello," said Pat. "It's a good thing you rang those bells. We were properly lost. Never mind – we're all right now."

"The good Lord will be our guide," said the Reverend Timms. "Come and have some tea; there's plenty in the pot."

"Thanks – I need it," said Pat. There was milk for Jess.

They talked of other foggy days they had known, and enjoyed their tea.

Then, Miss Hubbard said, "Look at the windows!" The coloured glass was shining quite brightly. "It's much brighter outside." They went to the door.

A breeze was blowing the fog away and the sun was beginning to shine. They could see the fields and hills again.

"That's *much* better," said Pat. "Now I can get on with my letters. Come on, Jess. Cheerio! Thanks for the tea!"

Pat waved goodbye and went on his way. It was lovely driving along in the sunshine, without getting lost. They passed the scarecrow, standing patiently in its field.

"Look, Jess," said Pat. "That scarecrow's still waiting for a letter."

Jess was hoping there would be rabbit-pie for tea.